The Pet Person

For D.A.W. – J.W.

First published in Great Britain by Andersen Press Ltd in 1996
First published in Picture Lions in 1997
1 3 5 7 9 10 8 6 4 2
ISBN: 0 00 664597 6
Picture Lions is an imprint of the Children's Division,
part of HarperCollins Publishers Ltd,
77-85 Fulham Palace Road, Hammersmith, London W6 8JB.
Text copyright © Jeanne Willis 1996
Illustrations copyright © Tony Ross 1996
The author and illustrator assert the moral right to be identified
as the author and illustrator of the work.
Printed and bound in Hong Kong.

Barking by Jeanne Willis
Scratching by Tony Ross

Taken for Walkies by

PictureLions

An Imprint of HarperCollins*Publishers*

"What do you want for your birthday, Rex?"
"A pet person," said Rex.
"No, it'll ruin the furniture," said his mother.

"It won't," said Rex,
"I'll take it for walks."
"I'm not arguing," she said.
Rex went to find his father.

"Can I have a pet person for my birthday?" asked Rex.

"No," said his father. "It would eat us out of house and home. Anyway, they smell."

"Not if you look after them properly," said Rex.
"*I'll* end up looking after it," said his father.
"The answer is NO!"
Rex went to see Uncle Fido.
"People make lousy pets," said Uncle Fido. "They can be vicious. What if it attacked your little sister?"

Rex shrugged.
"I'll train it not to,"
he said.

"They are impossible to train," said his Auntie Sheba.

Rex decided to ask his grandfather.

"The trouble with young dogs today," growled Grandfather, "is that they want it all."

"I don't," said Rex, "all I want is a person to call my own."

"Why can't you make do with a new bone, like anyone else?" snapped his grandfather. "Horrible things, people."

"Yes," said his grandmother. "They're sweet when they are little, but when they grow up, they develop embarrassing habits."

"Like what?" asked Rex.

"Oh, eating at the table, that sort of thing," whispered Grandma.

"Talk about giving a person a bad name," thought Rex.

He went to the park, sat at the top of a hill and sulked.

Down below, dogs were walking their people.
The people were all shapes and sizes. Pedigrees with
fine coats, mongrelly ones, old ones, fat ones, thin ones.

"It's not fair," thought Rex. "How come those dogs are allowed to have a pet person, and I'm not?"
Then he saw a little ginger one all by itself.
It looked lonely.

"Poor thing," thought Rex. "Maybe it's a stray."
"Here, boy...here, Ginger!" he said, hoping it wouldn't bite.
It came over. It patted Rex on the head.

"There's a good person," said Rex. "Now, sit!"
But the person wanted to play.

It was fun at first. But then it got a bit frisky.
It would keep jumping in the mud!

It was noisy.

It frightened the ducks.

It kept wanting to be fed.

And it kept running off and getting into fights.

It followed Rex everywhere.
"Go home, Ginger. I can't keep you!"
said Rex. "Shoo!"
But the naughty person
wouldn't go.

A woman opened
her front door.
She looked at Rex
and frowned.
"Don't play with
that scruffy-looking
thing. He'll give
you *fleas*,"
she said.

"WILL HE?" said Rex,
looking at the boy in horror.
"Thanks for the
warning."

Rex ran home—he didn't want fleas. He'd gone right off the idea of having a pet person.

"Guess what we've got for your birthday," said his mother.

"I do hope it's a tennis ball," sighed Rex.

"No," she said. "But it *is* round and bouncy!"

Collins
Picture Lions

Have you read all these stories by Tony Ross?

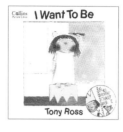
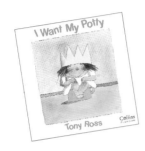
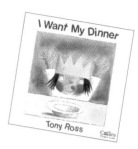
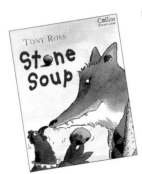

 Listen out for these stories on tape:

I WANT MY POTTY • I WANT TO BE • I WANT MY DINNER • STONE SOUP • RECKLESS RUBY